P9-AFQ-648

DEDICATION

To the wisdom revealed by all Great Teachers:
The Kingdom of Heaven is within you.
The truth shall set you free.

Cornelius
and the
Dog Star

By Diana Spyropulos
Illustrated by Ray Williams

ornelius Basset-Hound, citizen of Dogberry County, did not believe in playing games or having adventures. He believed in what was useful and what would help his corn grow tall and sweet.

Cornelius and his wife, Cherie, lived in a grand old farmhouse, together with their eleven grown puppies and twenty-seven grandpuppies.

 ornelius had many admirable qualities. He was honest, hard-working and dependable. Unfortunately, he was also quite a grouch. Whenever the grandpuppies played noisy games, he would sternly shake his paw and bark, "Puppies should be seen and not heard!" And when his grown puppies gathered to sing under the rising moon, Cornelius would complain, "What a silly waste of time."

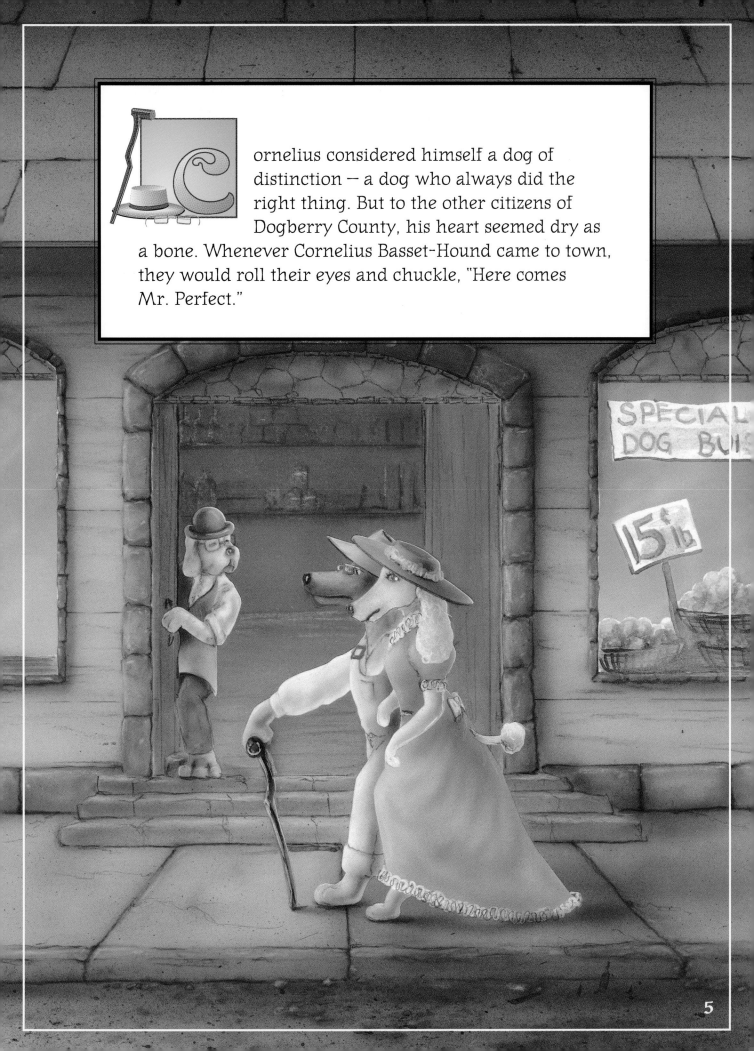

ornelius considered himself a dog of distinction — a dog who always did the right thing. But to the other citizens of Dogberry County, his heart seemed dry as a bone. Whenever Cornelius Basset-Hound came to town, they would roll their eyes and chuckle, "Here comes Mr. Perfect."

I n her younger days, Cherie had been a famous show dog. She still loved to sing and dance as she cared for their growing family.

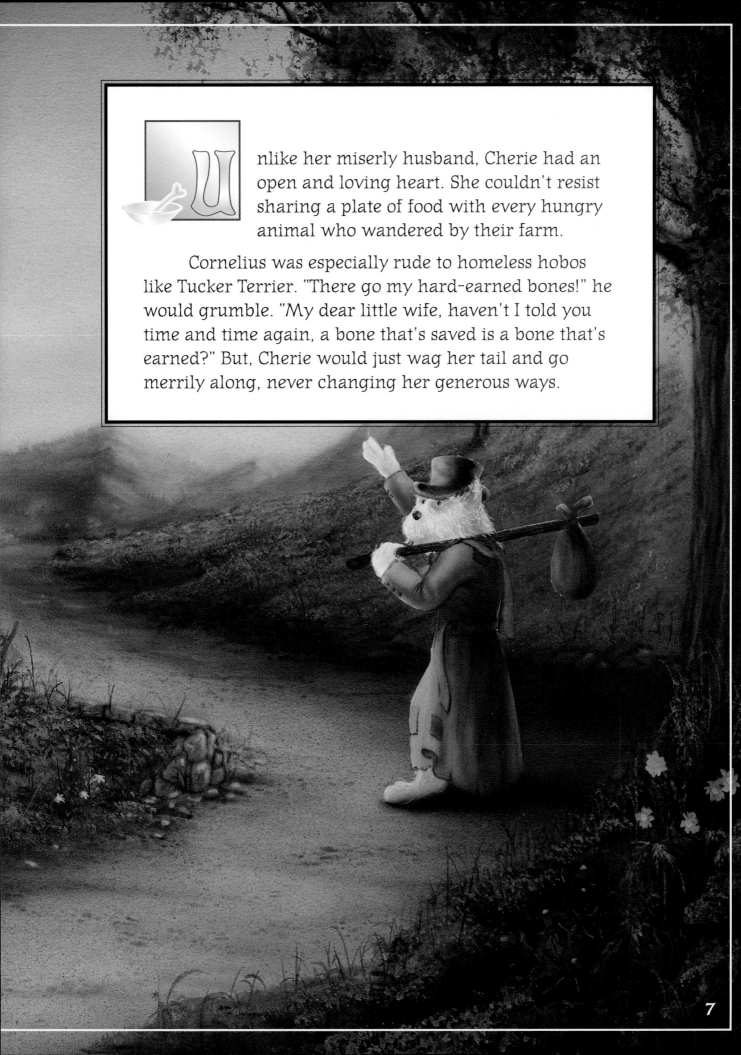

nlike her miserly husband, Cherie had an open and loving heart. She couldn't resist sharing a plate of food with every hungry animal who wandered by their farm.

Cornelius was especially rude to homeless hobos like Tucker Terrier. "There go my hard-earned bones!" he would grumble. "My dear little wife, haven't I told you time and time again, a bone that's saved is a bone that's earned?" But, Cherie would just wag her tail and go merrily along, never changing her generous ways.

efore he knew it, Cornelius had grown very, very old. He now spent most of his time sitting quietly on the porch, gazing out at his beloved fields. "I can hardly believe it's true," he would remind himself. "I, Cornelius Basset-Hound, shall soon be gone."

But, he wasn't really worried about dying. Cornelius was sure as the fur on his snout that a very special place was reserved for him in Dog Heaven.

hese days, when the youngsters scampered noisily through the house, old Cornelius would weakly lift a paw and mumble, "Puppies should be heard and not saved... I mean, a save that's earned...a earn that's boned..."

"Yes dear, a bone that's saved is a bone that's earned," Cherie would whisper, kissing him ever so gently on his long snout.

 ne summer evening, as millions of stars glittered across the sky, Cornelius Basset-Hound nodded off in his easy chair and sighed his last breath. Suddenly, he was floating near the ceiling, looking down at his own body. At first, it seemed like the strangest dream. Then he gasped, "This isn't a dream! I'm dead!"

 ornelius was swept upward into a brilliant tunnel of light, swirling higher and higher above the Earth. Then the astonished basset hound – who had never ventured beyond Dogberry County, even once – found himself flying past the silvery moon, through the Milky Way and straight to the towering gates of Dog Heaven.

efore the heavenly gates stood Saint Bernard, arrayed in shimmering robes and crowned with a golden halo. Above him, a Canine Choir was singing glorious celestial hymns.

 fter joining the long line of new arrivals, Cornelius looked around. "This is a much scruffier lot of dogs than I expected to find at the gates of Heaven. I can't wait to see the special place that's reserved for me!"

lancing back, Cornelius was surprised to see a familiar face. "Why, that's Tucker Terrier," he grumbled. "Cherie used to give my hard-earned bones to that old beggar. What is he doing here?"

hen Cornelius reached the front of the line, Saint Bernard looked down at his official scrolls, slowly shook his head and sighed, "Oh...it's you."

"Yes sir, I am Cornelius Basset-Hound of Dogberry County!"

"That's right...and you are not ready to enter Heaven."

"There must be some mistake," Cornelius gasped. "What do you mean I'm not ready?"

"Well, for one thing, you are no fun. Who wants to spend eternity with a miserly old grouch?" replied Saint Bernard.

"But, all my life I was a dog of distinction," cried Cornelius. "I always tried to do my duty."

"What about love? What about kindness, Cornelius Basset-Hound? To enter Heaven you must open your heart and learn to show your love."

Scratching his head in terrible confusion, Cornelius slowly wandered away. "But I don't understand. What does he mean, open my heart?"

ornelius looked back and was amazed to see Tucker floating blissfully through the heavenly gates. "What's going on here?" groaned the dazed basset hound. "He's nothing but a bum!"

hile resting on a little cloud, Cornelius shook his head in disbelief, "Saint Bernard has made a terrible mistake. I did love my family. I wish, oh, I wish..."

"HAT DO YOU WISH?" a thundering voice rang from the heavens.

"I wish I could see my family," said Cornelius. Then, blinking with surprise, he barked, "Who are you?"

"I am Sirius, the Dog Star. How can I help you?"

Gazing into the blazing face of the Dog Star, Cornelius blurted, "I'm so confused. Nothing makes sense anymore. And I certainly don't like being dead!"

"Dead?" exclaimed Sirius. "How could you be talking with me if you were dead? Only your worn-out old body is gone. Tell me, do you miss it?"

Cornelius suddenly realized he hadn't felt the slightest ache or pain since leaving his old body. And his mind was perfectly clear. "A bone that's saved is a bone that's earned!" he shouted jubilantly.

"I beg your pardon?" asked the Dog Star. "You do seem a bit confused."

"Well, I need to correct a terrible mistake. Saint Bernard says I'm not ready to enter Heaven...that I'm a miserly old grouch. But if you could see how much my family misses me, then you'd know how wrong he is about me!"

"It is possible to see them," Sirius smiled. "Just wish with all your might."

 nd so, Cornelius wished and wished until, through the shining light of Sirius, he could see into every room of the old farmhouse. At first, he was overjoyed to see his family. But then, he couldn't believe his eyes!

Except for Cherie, no one looked even a little sad. The puppies were scampering around the house playing noisy games and silly tricks. It was perfectly clear that they didn't miss him at all.

"After everything I did for them." sobbed Cornelius. "Why don't they miss me? I loved them so much."

"Cornelius, my friend, you say you loved your family, but how did you show it?"

"By scolding them, of course," answered Cornelius. "By scolding them each and every day so they would always do the right thing!"

"Could that be why they don't miss you?" the Dog Star asked gently.

s his family and farm faded from view, Cornelius howled to the moons and the stars and the constellations. "It must be true. I was an old grouch! No wonder they don't miss me!" In a rush of tears, he cried, "I never once said I loved them. Not even to my dearest Cherie. Oh, Sirius, what shall I do?"

"ou must find the way to open your heart," whispered the Dog Star. "Now, my friend, the time has come for me to go."

"Please don't leave me!" pleaded Cornelius.

"The journey of your heart must be taken alone," the Dog Star's voice echoed as he soared off into a sea of stars.

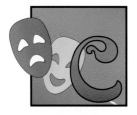

ornelius stared into the vast reaches of space and began trembling. Suddenly, he remembered the homeless dogs who passed through Dogberry County. "Is it possible," he asked himself, "that I've become a hobo, too?"

After gathering his courage, Cornelius began to wander through the endless skies. On and on he traveled, until one day, feeling so weary and alone, he cried out, "There must be a special place for me! Won't somebody please help me find it?"

Lost in his tears, Cornelius didn't notice that the stars were drawing closer together. When he finally looked up, a celestial message was blazing across the sky.

KNOW YOURSELF · LOVE YOURSELF

LOVE AND LAUGHTER ARE THE BEST MEDICINES

s Cornelius gazed at the sparkling stars, his sadness turned to joy. "Nothing can keep a good dog down!" he shouted, bounding off to continue his search.

 oon Cornelius came upon a shimmering
celestial city filled with magnificent parks,
buildings and fountains. Under a flowering
dogwood tree, a group of radiant, peaceful
dogs sat chatting about the wonders of the universe.
"Come join us," they called.

Cornelius joined them for awhile, but he hardly knew
what to do or say around these shining souls. "I don't feel
at home here," he told himself. "But, I do wish I was
more like them."

Then, right before his eyes, a glowing angel suddenly appeared. "I heard your wish," she said softly. "I know a place where you can learn many things."

Taking his paw, she led Cornelius silently through the heavens. When they stopped at the edge of a grassy meadow, the angel smiled, then vanished without a trace. Cornelius saw dozens of dogs laughing uproariously as they rolled around in the tall grass. "What's so funny?" he asked.

"We are learning to take ourselves lightly," a jovial bulldog replied. "On Earth, we were much too serious, so now we're making up for lost time. Come join us."

He soon felt right at home with the laughing dogs. They had long talks and lots of fun sharing stories about their stodgy lives. And, as Cornelius learned to laugh, his heart slowly began to open.

Although Cornelius enjoyed being with his new companions, whenever he thought about his life on Earth, he regretted having been such a stingy old grouch. "I was so busy trying to be Mr. Perfect that I never learned how to be a friend."

Cornelius missed his family more than ever. He started dreaming of ways to show them his love — like playing noisy games with his grandpuppies, singing under the rising moon with his grown puppies, or dancing cheek-to-cheek with Cherie.

Then his heart would swell with eagerness and joy, like the heart of a puppy. "Love never dies," he would whisper. "Nothing is deeper or sweeter or stronger than love."

he time came when Cornelius knew he must leave the grassy meadow to continue the journey of his heart. He felt an irresistible urge to climb the majestic cloud mountain that loomed in the distance.

Reaching the crest of the mountain, Cornelius discovered a garden that glowed with soft, pure light. Everywhere there were bright flowers, rainbow fountains and crystal pools. In the center of the garden he came upon a golden bowl engraved with his name. Inside the bowl there was a shining bone. "Everything here is so beautiful! Could this be my special place?"

ornelius was surprised to see a familiar dog trotting toward him. Despite his scruffy fur and tattered clothes, Tucker Terrier was a most welcome sight. "What are you doing here?" exclaimed Cornelius. "Not long ago, I saw you passing through the gates of Heaven."

"That was only the beginning of my journey. Since then, I've had the most amazing adventures," answered Tucker. "How about you?" This started a lively discussion.

In the glow of the garden, the two dogs sat happily together, sharing memories of their earthly lives and celestial adventures. Tucker wagged his tail and laughed, "Look at me. I still look like a hobo."

Cornelius couldn't help laughing too, because all he could see now was Tucker's loving heart. Taking the bone from his golden bowl, Cornelius broke it in two. As he offered the larger part to Tucker, his heart sang out, "A bone that's shared fills two hearts forever!"

fter saying goodbye to Tucker, Cornelius rested among the flowers. At the first light of dawn, he glanced into one of the reflecting pools. "Is that me?"

His whole body was glowing with light. Cornelius saw rays of divine love flowing from his heart. "Could it be true?" he wondered. "Is my own heart that special place I've been searching for?"

Looking around, he realized that this same divine light was shining in every flower, tree, and star. Cornelius Basset-Hound suddenly began dancing the most joyful jig ever seen in Heaven or on Earth.

"HAT A FINE DANCER YOU ARE!" rang a deep, familiar voice.

"Sirius! It's great to see you again!"

"How goes your journey?" asked the Dog Star. "What have you discovered?"

"After you left, I moped around for awhile," Cornelius admitted. "But since then I've had the greatest adventures. Once, a beautiful angel led me to a group of dogs who were a lot like me. I learned how to laugh, especially at myself.

"Then, I became friends with Tucker, one of the dogs I treated so poorly on Earth. What a splendid fellow he is. Oh, Sirius, it's so much better being a loving friend than a miserly old grouch!"

"Much better," Sirius agreed. "You have come far, Cornelius Basset-Hound, very far — and your heart has opened wide."

ow, my friend, it's time to discuss your future," Sirius continued. "Of course, you are free to remain here in the celestial realms for as long as you wish. You could choose to live on another planet... or you could rejoin your family on Earth."

"Wait! What do you mean rejoin my family?"

"You could be reborn this very afternoon," Sirius beamed, "as your own great-great-great-grandson. But remember, life on Earth can be very challenging, and..."

"I want to return to my family!" Cornelius interrupted with a shout that shook the heavens.

"Just as I thought!" laughed the Dog Star. "Of course, you will probably forget you were Cornelius Basset-Hound of Dogberry County — and that you have ever lived before.

"There is one more thing, dear friend. Do try to remember that you are never alone. Wherever you go, the Light of Heaven always shines inside your heart."

And so, at three o'clock that afternoon, a new litter of puppies arrived at the old farmhouse. Great-great-great grandmama Cherie felt especially drawn to one tiny fellow, whose markings looked very familiar. She asked that he be named Cornelius.

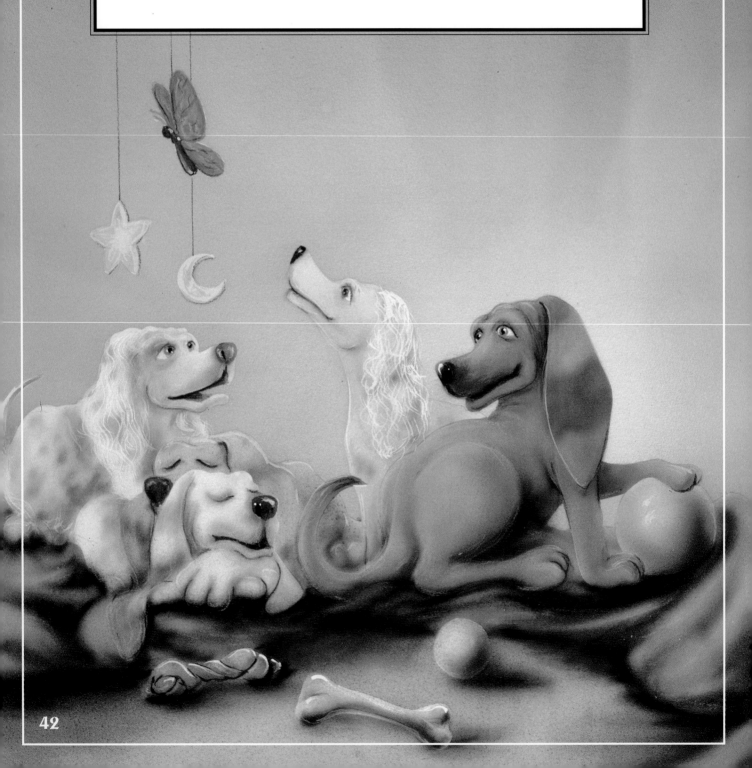

nd as Cornelius grew, his favorite thing to do was to make a dog or puppy's tail wag with happiness. The old farmhouse was more noisy and joyous than ever.

The floppy-eared pup loved being near his great-great-great-grandmama. Whenever they were alone, she would kiss him ever so gently on his little snout and whisper, "You are my joy and my comfort."

ne summer night when Cornelius was nearly grown, Cherie found him on the porch steps, searching the starry sky. "Come to bed, dear," she called. "You've been up almost half the night."

But Cornelius couldn't stop gazing at the moon and the stars and the constellations. He was trying to remember something, something about the sparkling heavens — and about himself — that he had once known.

All the while Sirius, the Dog Star, was winking and blinking the blessings of love upon him.

The End?

DIANA SPYROPULOS

"For my beloved children, Peter and Danielle, and my beloved
"wild-bird" mama, Katherine Spyropulos."

Diana was born and raised in New York City. Since graduating from New York University, she has been a high school English teacher, social worker, singer/songwriter and actress. Diana's songs have been recorded and performed on television, radio and in numerous nightclubs. She has published several poems, short stories and a social studies textbook.

Diana loves rainstorms, C.S. Lewis books and flying dreams. She lives in New York State with her children, Peter and Danielle, and their wise old cat, Aslan.

RAY WILLIAMS

"Dedicated to my son Dylan and his dog."

Ray was an "army brat," raised in exotic places, including Italy and Libya. His surreal approach to artistry reflects his lifelong fascination with the unique, unusual and bizarre – possibly stemming from his Irish-gypsy roots.

Ray's paintings frequently appear in art shows, science fiction/ fantasy magazines, books and galleries – often winning best-in-show and people's choice awards. His company, Village Idiot Artworks, is based in Longview, Washington, where he lives with his son, and Midnight, their 13-year-old black cat.

✦

"In addition to Diana Spyropulos and Ray Williams, I wish to acknowledge four very talented individuals for their invaluable contributions in the editing and production of this very special book: Ruth Thompson, Judy Tompkins, Alison McIntosh, and Arrieana Thompson."

John Michael Thompson, Editor

Text Copyright © 1995 by Diana Spyropulos

Illustrations Copyright © 1995 by Ray Williams

All rights reserved. No part of this book may be reproduced or utilized in any form or by any means, electronic or mechanical, including photocopying, recording, or by any information storage and retrieval system, without permission in writing from the publisher, except by a book reviewer who may quote brief passages in a review.

First edition published by

ILLUMINATION ARTS

PUBLISHING COMPANY, INC.

P.O. BOX 1865

BELLEVUE, WA 98009

TEL: (206) 822-8015

FAX: (206) 827-1213

Library of Congress Cataloging-in-Publication Data

Spyropulos, Diana.
Cornelius and the Dog Star / by Diana Spyropulos; illustrated by Ray Williams.
p. cm.
Summary: A grouchy, miserly old dog dies and is rejected at the gates of Dog Heaven. In a journey of discovery, he learns to open his heart and becomes generous and loving.
ISBN: 0-935699-08-2 : $15.95
[1. Conduct of life - Fiction. 2. Heaven - Fiction. 3. Dogs -Fiction.]
I. Williams, Ray, 1952- ill. II. Title.
PZ7.S7223Co 1995 [Fic] - dc20   94-32335   CIP   AC

Published in the United States of America
Printed by Tien Wah Press of Singapore
10 9 8 7 6 5 4 3 2 1

Book Designer: Molly Murrah

Illumination Arts books are distributed by
Atrium Publishing Group
Tel: 1-800-275-2606

These special children's books are available at fine bookstores everywhere. Or you may order directly from us:

CORNELIUS AND THE DOG STAR

by Diana Spyropulos, Hardcover $15.95
Cornelius, a grouchy old basset hound is turned away at the gates of Dog Heaven. During his delightful journey of self-discovery, he learns about generosity, kindness, playfulness and love.

ALL I SEE IS PART OF ME

by Chara M. Curtis, Hardcover $15.95
International bestseller
Through a series of illuminating experiences, a young child explores his world and awakens to his connection with all of life.

FUN IS A FEELING

by Chara M. Curtis, Hardcover $14.95
In this poetic journey, a child discovers the wonder of his imagination and learns to see the fun hidden in everyday life.

HOW FAR TO HEAVEN?

by Chara M. Curtis, Hardcover $15.95
During an enchanting walk through the woods, Nanna helps her granddaughter to see the signs of heaven in all of nature.

For shipping and handling add $3.00 for the first book and $.75 for each additional book. Washington residents please add 8.2% sales tax. VISA and Mastercard accepted.

ILLUMINATION ARTS
PUBLISHING COMPANY, INC.
P.O. BOX 1865
BELLEVUE, WA 98009
TEL: (206) 822-8015
FAX: (206) 827-1213